THE DRAGONSITTER'S Party

THE DRAGONSITTER'S Party

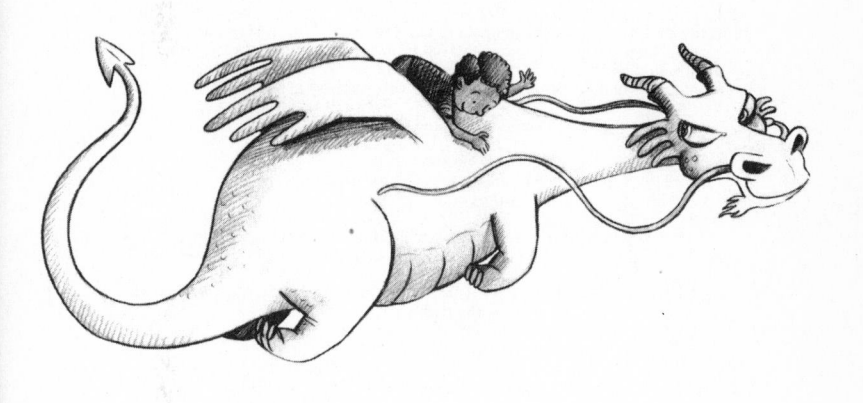

Josh Lacey

Illustrated by Garry Parsons

LITTLE, BROWN AND COMPANY
New York • Boston

Text copyright © 2015 by Josh Lacey
Illustrations copyright © 2015 by Garry Parsons
Text in excerpt from *The Dragonsitter to the Rescue*
copyright © 2016 by Josh Lacey
Illustrations from *The Dragonsitter to the Rescue*
copyright © 2016 by Garry Parsons

Little, Brown and Company

Hachette Book Group
1290 Avenue of the Americas, New York, NY 10104
Visit us at lb-kids.com

Little, Brown and Company is a division of Hachette Book Group, Inc.
The Little, Brown name and logo are trademarks of Hachette Book Group, Inc.

The publisher is not responsible for websites (or their content) that are not owned by the publisher.

First U.S. Hardcover Edition: January 2017
First U.S. Paperback Edition: January 2017
Originally published in Great Britain in 2015 by Andersen Press Limited

Library of Congress Control Number: 2016940681

ISBN 978-0-316-38243-4 (hc)—ISBN 978-0-316-29913-8 (pb)

10 9 8 7 6 5 4 3 2 1

LSC-C

Printed in the United States of America

THE DRAGONSITTER'S Party

ABRACADABRA!
KAZAM KAZOOM!!
PREPARE TO BE AMAZED!!!

The world-famous master of magic

Mister Mysterio

will be appearing at Eddie's birthday party

COME AND SEE HIS

INCREDIBLE TRICKS

YOU WILL NOT BELIEVE YOUR EYES!

At: Eddie's house

On: Saturday, March 25th   From: 3 p.m. to 5 p.m.

Please RSVP to: Eddie's mom

Dear Uncle Morton,

Did you get my invitation?

I just wanted to check because you're the only person who hasn't RSVPed.

I hope you can come. It's going to be a great party. We're having a magician.

Love from your favorite nephew,

Eddie

Dear Eddie,

I would have loved to come to your party. There is very little that I enjoy more than the work of a good magician.

Unfortunately, I have already promised to stay in Scotland and help on the farm with Mr. McDougall, who is a man short this weekend.

That man is, of course, our mutual friend Gordon, who is very excited about coming to see you. He talks about nothing else.

I can hardly believe that he only met your mother a few weeks ago. He already seems to know much more about her than I do, and I've known her for an entire lifetime.

Mr. McDougall only agreed to give Gordon the weekend off if I would work in his place. This is the farm's busiest time of the year, when all the new lambs are born.

He will be bringing a small birthday surprise for you.

With love from your affectionate uncle,

Morton

Dear Uncle Morton,

Thank you for the surprise. I can't wait to see what it is.

Mom is very excited about Gordon coming to visit. She keeps buying new dresses, then taking them back to the store because they're not quite right.

I'm sorry you can't come to my party. I know my friends would like to meet you. Will you come next year instead?

I'll send you some pictures of Mister Mysterio sawing someone in half.

Apparently that's the best part of his act.

I am going to suggest he pick Emily.

She said, "That's not funny," and I said I
wasn't trying to be funny. I just thought
the house would be a bit more peaceful
if I only had half a sister.

Love,

Eddie

From: Edward Smith-Pickle

To: Morton Pickle

Date: Thursday, March 23

Subject: Special time

 Attachments: They're here!

Dear Uncle Morton,

Gordon has arrived with your surprise.

Mom was definitely surprised, but not in a good way.

She said if she'd wanted your dragons to come and stay, she would have invited them.

She was hoping to spend some special time with Gordon this weekend, but she says their time isn't going to be very special if she's got to look after two dragons, not to mention the nineteen kids who will be descending on the house on Saturday afternoon.

Of course, I was very happy to see them.

I can't believe how much Arthur has grown!

He's also getting quite good at flying. We put him in the yard in case he needed to poop after the long drive, and he almost got over the fence.

It's lucky he didn't, because Mrs. Kapelski was pruning her roses and she has a weak heart.

I do wish Ziggy and Arthur could stay for my party. I know my friends would like to meet them.

But Mom said, "Not a chance, buster."

Could you come and get them ASAP?

Love,

Eddie

From: Edward Smith-Pickle

To: Morton Pickle

Date: Thursday, March 23

Subject: Dinner

Attachments: I don't do pets

Dear Uncle Morton,

I just called both your numbers, but there was no answer. Are you already on your way to collect the dragons?

I hope so, because Mom says they are living on borrowed time.

She and Gordon were supposed to go out for dinner at a fancy French restaurant. Mom was wearing her best new dress, and Gordon looked very nice in his suit.

But the babysitter took one look at Arthur and said, "I don't do pets."

We promised to lock Arthur upstairs in my bedroom with Ziggy, but she wouldn't change her mind, even when Mom offered to pay her double.

By that time it was too late to get another babysitter, so Mom had to cancel the reservation.

Luckily, she had two steaks in the fridge, so they decided to stay here and have a nice romantic evening in front of the TV.

Unluckily, she took the steaks out of the fridge, put them on the counter, and turned around to get the vegetables.

By the time she turned back again, Ziggy had eaten one steak and Arthur was halfway through the other.

So she's ordered some curry.

Gordon says he likes curry much more than French food, but I think he's just trying to be nice.

Please call us ASAP and tell us your ETA.

Eddie

P.S. If you don't know what ETA means, it means Estimated Time of Arrival.

Dear Uncle Morton,

Arthur ate the curry.

I didn't actually see it happen because I was upstairs brushing my teeth, but I heard the screams.

Mom says if you're not here first thing tomorrow morning, she's going to put your dragons on the train and send them back to Scotland on their own.

To be honest, I can understand why she's so upset.

She's been looking forward to her date with Gordon for ages, and your dragons have just ruined it.

She won't even let them in the house now.

She chased them onto the patio with a broom and said they have to stay there all night.

I wanted to stay out there with them in my sleeping bag, but Mom says I'll catch my death of cold.

I hope the dragons don't catch theirs.

Eddie

Dear Eddie,

I'm terribly sorry I haven't replied to your recent messages, but it's all hands on deck for the lambing here.

Please tell your mother that I am very sorry. I had thought the dragons would be a nice birthday surprise for you. I didn't realize that they would spoil her weekend with Gordon.

Of course I will come and collect them. I have just checked the train schedule. If I leave my island at dawn and row to the mainland, I can get to the station in time for the first train and should be with you by the evening.

However, I have already promised my services to Mr. McDougall for the entire weekend, so I can only leave him in the lurch if Gordon comes straight back here and does the lambing himself.

Unless your mother would prefer him to stay where he is?

Morton

P.S. Your mother is quite right: However warm your sleeping bag may be, you will be much more comfortable in your own bed. There is no need to be concerned about Ziggy and Arthur. They are used to Scottish winters and Outer Mongolian blizzards, so a short time in the yard won't do them any harm.

Dear Uncle Morton,

I told Mom what you said. She thought about it for a bit. Then she said, "Fine."

I think she must really like Gordon.

Mom even let the dragons back inside.

I just hope the smell doesn't make her change her mind.

Arthur has been making terrible farts all morning. The whole house stinks like curry.

He'd better stop before tomorrow or my friends will be poisoned.

Now they're having oatmeal for breakfast.

I wouldn't have thought dragons liked oatmeal, but yours seem to.

Gordon says no one could possibly resist proper oatmeal made by a real Scotsman.

Even I quite liked it, and I hate oatmeal.

I'd better go now. It's time for school.

I wish I could stay here and make cupcakes with Gordon.

But Mom says life isn't fair, even on the day before your birthday.

Love,

Eddie

P.S. Emily asks if you can send a picture of the lambs.

P.P.S. Please say hello to Mr. McDougall from me.

From: Edward Smith-Pickle

To: Morton Pickle

Date: Friday, March 24

Subject: Where are you????

 Attachments: Quiet night in; Popcorn problem

Dear Uncle Morton,

Mom says thanks very much for ruining her one chance at happiness.

Gordon has gone for a walk. He said, "See you later," but Mom says he'll probably just drive straight back to Scotland.

I think they had a bit of a fight.

It was Ziggy's fault. Or maybe Arthur's.

I don't know which of them bit the babysitter.

Mom found one who also watches pets. She booked another table at that French restaurant. She was wearing her second-favorite dress, and Gordon was in his suit again.

Emily and I waved good-bye from the doorstep.

Then we stayed here and watched TV with the babysitter.

Everything was going fine until the babysitter got hungry.

She should have known you never take popcorn from a dragon.

When the smoke cleared, the babysitter was jumping around on one leg, screaming at the top of her lungs, and looking for her phone.

Mom and Gordon had to come straight home. They didn't even get to try their appetizer.

Now Ziggy and Arthur are back on the patio.

They both look very sad.

They're staring through the glass, watching Mom eat their malted milk balls.

She's going to put them on the train to Scotland if you're not here first thing tomorrow morning.

I don't like the idea of two dragons alone on the train, but Mom says they're old enough to look after themselves.

Please get here soon.

Eddie

Dear Eddie,

You can tell your mother not to worry.
I have just booked a flight from Glasgow,
leaving at nine o'clock tomorrow morning.
I should be with you just after lunch.

I am very much looking forward to wishing
you a happy birthday in person.

If your mother will allow me and the
dragons to stay for the afternoon, I will
have a chance to see your magician in
action.

Unfortunately, I appear to have misplaced
your invitation. Can you remind me what
time the party starts?

Finally—and most importantly—what would you like for your birthday? I'm ashamed to say that I have failed to buy you anything, but if you could give me a suggestion for the perfect gift, I shall try to find it at the airport.

Love from your affectionate uncle,

Morton

Dear Uncle Morton,

The party starts at three o'clock.

Please try to get here on time or you'll miss Mister Mysterio sawing someone in half.

I'm very pleased my friends will get to meet you.

Don't worry about not getting me a birthday present. Dad didn't, either.

He didn't even send me a card. He just texted me this morning.

Mom said that was typical of him, which isn't actually true because last year he sent me a new bike.

27

I think he's just very busy at the moment rebuilding his castle.

If you would like to get me something, I would really like a magic set.

I did ask Mom for one, but she gave me a microscope and a book and another book and three pairs of socks instead.

Gordon gave me a fishing rod.

I always thought fishing was a bit boring, but he says nothing could be further from the truth.

He wanted to teach me this morning, but Mom said not when nineteen kids are arriving any minute.

They're not really arriving any minute. It's only ten past eight.

But we do have a lot of cleaning up to do before the party starts, not to mention making the sandwiches, opening the bags of chips, and putting all the pigs in a blanket on plates.

So I'd better go.

See you later!

Love,

Eddie

From: Edward Smith-Pickle

To: Morton Pickle

Date: Saturday, March 25

Subject: My party

Attachments: Party pics

Dear Uncle Morton,

Did you miss your flight?

You missed a great party, too.

I thought it was great, anyway, although I'm not sure everyone did.

Mister Mysterio certainly didn't.

The problem was he didn't listen to me.

The first part of his act went really well. First, he made a coin disappear. Then he found it behind Emily's ear.

I said I could do that, too.

Then he made ten coins disappear and he pulled a ten-dollar bill out of Emily's nose.

He said, "Can you do that?"

I said I couldn't.

Then he asked me to pick a card, any card.

It was the Queen of Hearts.

He let me put the card back in the deck and shuffle it.

Then he took the deck and threw it in the air and just caught one of the cards—and it was the Queen of Hearts!

Then he made
a real goldfish
appear in a glass
of water.

Then he drank it
and the goldfish
appeared in
another glass.

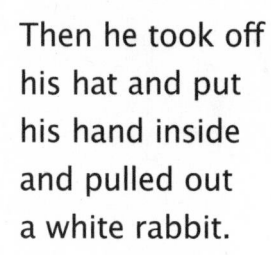

Then he took off
his hat and put
his hand inside
and pulled out
a white rabbit.

I knew what would happen next. I had to warn Mister Mysterio. I shouted at him, "Put the rabbit back in the hat!"

"That's my next trick," he said. "First, Henrietta is going to make some lettuce disappear."

He reached into his pocket and pulled out a handful of lettuce.

"*Bon appétit*, Henrietta," he said, and gave the lettuce to the rabbit.

I shouted, "Look out! Behind you!"

Mister Mysterio just smiled. He said, "This is a magic show, not a pantomime. Let Henrietta eat her lettuce in peace."

She can't have taken more than a nibble before Ziggy swallowed her.

One gulp and she was gone.

For a moment, everyone was too surprised to speak.

Then Mister Mysterio went red in the face and started shouting at the top of his lungs.

Mom said a self-respecting children's entertainer ought to be ashamed of himself for using language like that.

Mister Mysterio just shouted even louder.

He wanted Mom to pay eight hundred dollars to replace Henrietta.

Apparently it takes years to train a rabbit.

Emily asked if he was such a good magician, why couldn't he magic the rabbit back again?

I thought that was actually a good suggestion, but Mister Mysterio did not care.

He said if Mom didn't write him a check for eight hundred dollars plus his usual fee and expenses *right now this minute*, he was going to call the police.

I think he really would have if Gordon hadn't taken him aside and spoken to him.

I don't know what Gordon said, but Mister Mysterio went very quiet. He packed his suitcase and left without even saying good-bye.

I said maybe he could come back next year to saw Emily in half, and Mom said next year we're going to the movies instead.

After that we should have had snack time, but snack time was canceled because the dragons had eaten everything.

The kitchen door was supposed to be kept shut at all times, but Mister Mysterio must have left it open when he grabbed his coat.

The dragons didn't leave anything, not even a single pig in a blanket.

Arthur even ate the candles from the top of the cake.

Luckily, none of my friends minded,
because we went into the yard and Ziggy let
us take turns flying on her back.

Mom said please don't go too high or
someone will fall off and she'll never be able
to show her face at the playground again.

Ziggy did not listen. She flew my friend
Sam to the roof of the house and left him
there for twenty minutes while she was
flying the rest of us around.

When Sam came down, he said it was the
best birthday party ever.

I thought so, too.

Love from your one–year–older–than–yesterday nephew,

Eddie

From: Morton Pickle

To: Edward Smith-Pickle

Date: Saturday, March 25

Subject: Re: My party

Dear Eddie,

You must imagine me clearing my throat and taking a deep breath, then bursting into song:

> *Happy birthday to you,*
> *Happy birthday to you,*
> *Happy birthday, dear Eddie,*
> *Happy birthday to you!*

I am so sorry to have missed your party. We had a situation with one of the sheep last night, so it was impossible for me to catch my train to the airport this morning.

However, you will be glad to hear that her two lambs were delivered in perfect health just after nine o'clock this morning.

I have called them Eddie and Emily in your honor.

I have just looked at the trains and the flights. I could travel south tomorrow morning, but I would arrive at your house just as Gordon was leaving, which seems more than a little ridiculous. Would you mind looking after the dragons for one more night? Then he could bring them home in his car.

I have not forgotten your magic set, and I shall send it ASAP.

With much love and many happy returns from your affectionate uncle,

Morton

Dear Uncle Morton,

I hope you haven't bought me a magic set for my birthday, because I don't want one after all.

I've decided I don't like magicians.

Today, there was a knock at the door. It was Mister Mysterio.

He said he'd come for his money.

He kept shouting and waving his arms in the air.

Gordon said, "Why don't we calm down and talk about this like sensible people?"

Mister Mysterio said he'd had enough talking. He just wanted his money.

Mom said he had to leave right now or she was going to call the police.

Mister Mysterio said he'd already done that himself, but they weren't interested. They told him that if he called them with any more stories about rabbits and dragons, they would arrest him for wasting police time.

He said we'd have to sort this out between ourselves.

He said he wasn't going anywhere until we paid him.

He said he'd stay here all week if he had to.

He probably would have if Ziggy hadn't come to see what all the fuss was about.

That was when I realized Mister Mysterio wasn't a real magician.

A real magician would know it's not a good idea to shove a dragon.

For a moment, Ziggy stayed absolutely still.

All that moved was the smoke trickling out of her nostrils.

Then she went wild.

Mister Mysterio ran down the street with his butt on fire.

Gordon says he won't be coming back in a hurry.

Mom is worried he will, so she's asked Gordon to stay one more night.

She asks, can you carry on lambing?

Love,

Eddie

Dear Eddie,

Please tell your mother that I am actually tremendously busy at the moment and can hardly spare any time away from my desk.

I should be preparing for my next trip abroad. I will be traveling to Tibet to search for the yeti.

If Gordon is unable to return to Scotland tonight, I shall of course put my work aside and return to the lambs.

But I would be grateful if he could hurry home as soon as possible.

Morton

From: Edward Smith-Pickle

To: Morton Pickle

Date: Monday, March 27

Subject: ETD

Attachments: Packing

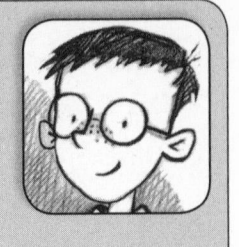

Dear Uncle Morton,

You'll be glad to hear Gordon is loading his car now, and his ETD is 8:15 a.m.

Mom is making him a thermos of extra-strong coffee and some sandwiches.

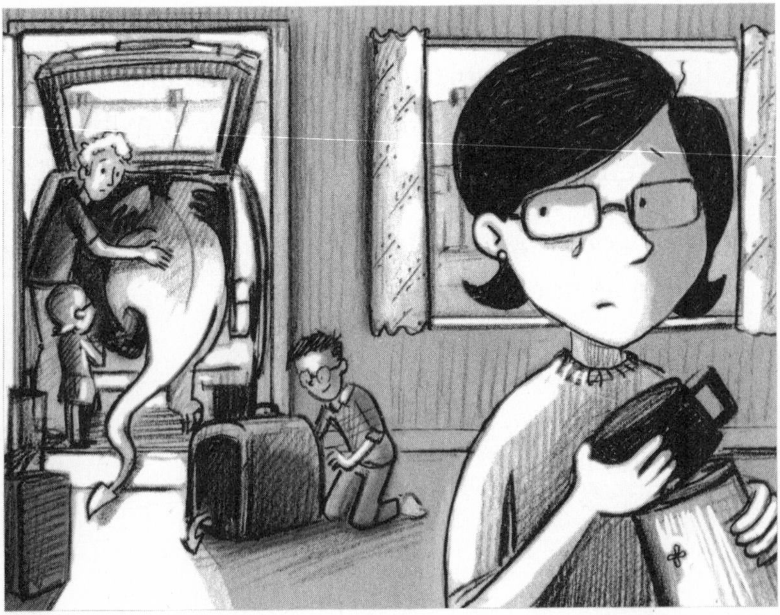

I've made goody bags for Ziggy and Arthur.

They've got chocolate bars, gummy bears, soda bottles, and sparkling lemonade.

Gordon is going to drive all day. If the traffic isn't too bad, he and the dragons should be home in time for dinner.

Love,

Eddie

P.S. If you don't know what ETD means, it means Estimated Time of Departure.

P.P.S. Emily says please don't forget the photo of the lambs.

P.P.P.S. Your trip to Tibet sounds very interesting. Can I come, too? I've always wanted to see a yeti.

P.P.P.P.S. Have you ever read an e-mail with so many P.S.s?

Dear Eddie,

I'm very pleased to report that the dragons are safely back at home. As I write, Ziggy and Arthur are lying on the carpet at my feet, looking as happy as happy can be.

Junk food obviously suits them. I have rarely seen either of them looking so healthy. I shall have to ask Mrs. McPherson at the post office to start stocking gummy bears.

Mr. McDougall was delighted to see Gordon and sent him straight out to work in the fields. I believe he has delivered three lambs already.

I attached a picture for Emily.

You can tell her that these two lambs were helped into the world by her uncle and are now wandering happily around Mr. McDougall's fields.

For you, my dear nephew, I have put a small birthday present in the mail. I'm sorry that it will be a couple of days late, but I hope you'll enjoy it anyway.

Thanks again for looking after the dragons so well.

With love from your affectionate uncle,

Morton

Dear Uncle Morton,

Thank you for the egg!

It's my best birthday present.

In fact, I think it's my best present ever.

I know you said it probably won't hatch, but I'm going to leave it in my sock drawer anyway.

Then if a dragon does come out, it will be nice and cozy.

Please say hello to Ziggy and Arthur from me. I hope you're keeping them away from the lambs.

Emily says thank you for the picture and she has never seen anything so cute.

Mom is a bit sad. I think she's missing Gordon. If you see him, please ask him to come visit us again soon.

The dragons are invited, too, of course.

Love,

Eddie

Barnacle, Mullet & Crabbe
Attorneys-at-Law

147 Lordship Lane, London EC1V 2AX
bcrabbe@barnaclemulletcrabbe.com

Thursday, March 30

Dear Mr. Pickle,

I have been instructed by my client, Barry Daniels, also known as The Amazing Mister Mysterio, to pursue a claim for damages against you and your pet or pets.

Our client was booked to perform a magic show at the birthday party of Edward Smith-Pickle on Saturday, March 25.

He had performed a little less than half of his usual routine when a creature, species unknown, pushed him aside and ate his rabbit, Henrietta.

Our client has been informed that the creature belongs to you, and therefore you bear full responsibility for its actions and its consequences.

Our client will accept a minimum payment of eight hundred dollars for the loss of his rabbit.

Henrietta had undergone two years of intensive training and had assisted our client in more than seventy magic shows. His business has been severely disrupted by her loss.

Our client also wishes to be reimbursed for his full fee and expenses for the magic show.

Finally, our client wishes to be reimbursed for one pair of brown trousers, which were damaged in a fire caused by your pet or pets.

A bill is enclosed.

Our client would be grateful for the full sum of the payment within seven days.

Yours sincerely,

Bartholomew Crabbe

Senior Partner
Barnacle, Mullet & Crabbe

Dear Mr. Crabbe,

Thank you for your letter about your client, Barry Daniels, also known as The Amazing Mister Mysterio.

I was very sorry to hear about Henrietta and her unfortunate accident. As an animal lover myself, I can appreciate how upsetting it must have been for your client.

I will, of course, provide him with a replacement, although I would rather not pay eight hundred dollars. That does seem awfully expensive for a rabbit, however well-trained.

I have an abundance of rabbits on my island. They are always eating my lettuce. Mister Mysterio is welcome to take as many as he wants.

Perhaps he could teach me some magic at the same time.

I have spoken to my sister, who told me that she has already sent a check to Mr. Daniels for his fee and expenses.

I suggested that she should only pay half his fee, since he only performed half his magic, but she has paid the full amount.

If I were Mr. Daniels, I should think myself very lucky.

With all best wishes,

Morton Pickle

Party Cupcakes

Gordon doesn't just make tasty oatmeal—he's also a star baker! Ask an adult to help you make these delicious cupcakes the next time you're having a party.

You will need:

- 1 cup butter, softened
- 1 cup granulated sugar
- 2 large eggs, beaten (chicken, not dragon)
- 1 teaspoon vanilla extract
- 1 cup flour, sifted
- 1 teaspoon baking powder
- 1-2 tablespoons of milk
- Icing tubes
- Silver candy balls
- Measuring cups and spoons
- Cupcake pan with 12 cups
- Baking cups
- Bowl
- Hand mixer
- Wooden spoon
- Oven
- Oven mitts
- Toothpick

1. Preheat the oven to 350°F and line the pan with baking cups.

2. Beat the butter and sugar together in a bowl with the hand mixer until pale and creamy.

3. Dribble in the beaten egg slowly as you mix. Then add the vanilla extract.

4. Add the flour and baking powder. Use the wooden spoon to mix thoroughly.

5. Add a little milk to make the mixture a bit more runny. It should drop off a spoon.

6. Divide the mixture between the cups, making sure they are only half full.

7. Get an adult to help you put the pan in the oven. Bake for 12–15 minutes, until the cupcakes are light brown and have risen to the top of the pan.

8. Wearing oven mitts, take the cupcakes out of the oven and test one with a toothpick—if it comes out clean, the cake is done. Remove the cupcakes from the pan after 10 minutes and leave to cool on a rack for a couple of hours.

9. Now you can have fun decorating your cupcakes! Why not use a green icing tube to draw a fierce dragon head and use silver candy balls for eyes?

What's next for Eddie, Ziggy & Arthur?

Don't miss their sixth adventure!

Turn the page for a sneak peek.

COMING SOON

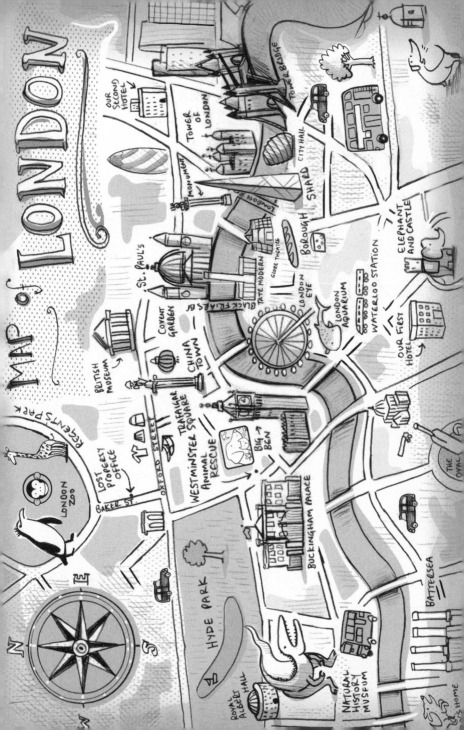

From: Edward Smith-Pickle

To: Morton Pickle

Date: Saturday, April 15

Subject: We've arrived!

Attachments: View; That's my bed!

Dear Uncle Morton,

Here is the view from our hotel window. If you look very closely, you can see Big Ben.

As you can also see, your dragons are fine.
They both had a good dinner. Now they're
fast asleep.

Dad didn't actually want to bring them.
He asked Mom to take them to Paris, but
she said, "No way." She said she didn't want
two badly behaved dragons spoiling her
romantic weekend with Gordon.

Dad said wasn't a romantic weekend in Paris a bit of a cliché, and Mom said she'd rather have a cliché than nothing at all, which was all *he* used to give her.

Gordon looked really embarrassed while they were shouting at one another, but Emily and I didn't mind. We're used to it.

Mom won. So the dragons are here. I have brought the egg, too, just in case it hatches. I wouldn't want a new dragon to arrive in an empty house.

I have to go now. Dad says it's bedtime. First thing tomorrow morning we're visiting the Natural History Museum.

Emily wants to go on the London Eye, which is a huge Ferris wheel, instead, but Dad says we'll do that the day after.

I hope you're having fun in Tibet. Have you seen the yeti yet?

Love,

Eddie

Dear Uncle Morton,

I have to tell you some bad news.

We have lost Arthur.

He's somewhere in London, but I don't know where.

Today, we went to the Natural History Museum. I've always wanted to go there, so I was *really* excited.

The only problem was Dad said the dragons had to stay in the hotel without us.

I said that was very unfair, but Dad said he wanted to spend some quality time with his children, not a pair of fire-breathing lizards. He said we could take them to a park later if they needed to stretch their wings.

He absolutely, definitely, no-question-about-it refused to change his mind.

So I hid Arthur in my backpack.

I knew I shouldn't have, but I couldn't stop myself.

I told him to be quiet in there. He *was,* on the subway. Very. And he carried on being quiet in the café where we stopped for a morning snack. I dropped some croissant through the top of the backpack, which seemed to keep him happy.

He even stayed quiet in the museum. He didn't make a squeak while we looked at the birds and the bears and the earthworms and the giraffe and the rhino and the dodo and the dolphin and the blue whale.

But when we got to the T. rex, he wriggled out of my backpack and flew off to have a look. Maybe he thought it was a long-lost cousin.

He flew the entire length of the T. rex from tail to head and landed on its nostrils. People were pointing and shouting and taking pictures.

Dad asked, "Where did that come from?"

I pretended I didn't know.

Guards came running. One of them said, "You're not allowed to have flying toys inside the museum."

I explained, "He's not a toy, he's a dragon."

The guard said he didn't care what it was,
I just had to get it out of here right now,
this minute, before he called the police and
had us all thrown out for making a public
nuisance of ourselves.

I said I would if I could catch him.

The guard got on his walkie-talkie and
called for reinforcements.

Unfortunately, catching Arthur was easier
said than done. He jumped off the T. rex

and whooshed over our heads, waggling his wings.

I ran after him. So did Dad and Emily and lots of guards.

Arthur was faster than any of us. He flew along the corridors, looped the loop around some statues, dive-bombed a crowd of Japanese tourists, and disappeared through the revolving doors. By the time we got outside, he had vanished.

We searched for hours, but we couldn't find him anywhere.

I wanted to keep on looking all night, but Dad said we'd just be wasting our time. So we came back to the hotel.

Ziggy was fast asleep. She still is. I don't know what I'm going to say to her when she wakes up.

Dad says if I was so concerned about the dragons, I shouldn't have hidden Arthur in my backpack in the first place. I suppose he's right.

I'm really sorry, Uncle Morton.

This whole thing is my fault, and I wish I knew how to make it better.

Eddie

Dear Uncle Morton,

I'm very sorry, but I've got some more bad news.

I've lost your other dragon, too.

Emily and I were brushing our teeth in the bathroom when we heard a terrible racket coming from the bedroom.

We rushed out of the bathroom and found Ziggy going wild. She was trying to break through the windows and get onto the balcony. She must have realized Arthur had gone missing.

Dad was standing on his bed, holding a pillow. He yelled at me to do something.

I didn't want to let her out, but there really wasn't any choice. One more minute and she would have smashed the whole place to pieces.

So I opened the door.

Ziggy charged onto the balcony, flapped her wings, and took off.

A moment later, she'd disappeared into the night.

I feel awful. I can't believe I've lost both your dragons. I wish I knew how to find them.

Do you have any brilliant ideas?

Dad says there's no point in writing to you because you won't be checking your e-mails in Tibet, but I hope you get this message.

Please write back if you do.

Eddie

From: Edward Smith–Pickle

To: Morton Pickle

Date: Monday, April 17

Subject: 8,000,000

Attachments: Londoners

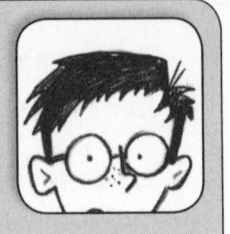

Dear Uncle Morton,

Your dragons are still missing.

We spent the whole day walking around London, but we didn't see any sign of them.

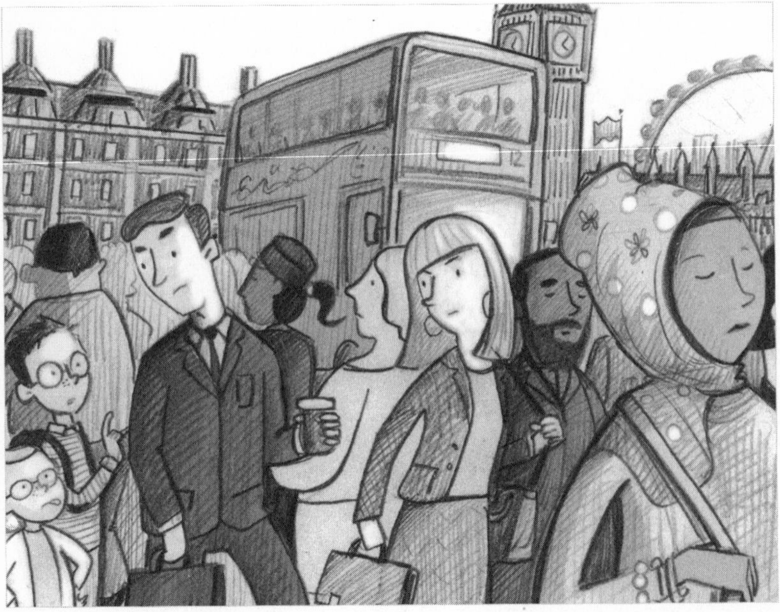

This city is so big!

Dad says eight million people live here. I think we met most of them.

I asked everyone if they'd seen a missing dragon. Some of them laughed. Others just walked past as if they couldn't even hear me.

People who live in London are quite rude. Dad says it's the same in all big cities. Emily wanted to know if Paris is like this, too, and Dad said it's even worse.

I hope Mom and Gordon are having more fun than us.

Love,

Eddie

Dear Uncle Morton,

We spent today searching for your dragons again, but we still haven't found them.

Dad says not to worry—they'll come back on their own good time.

He says this is our one chance to spend a few days in London and we should be making the most of it, missing dragons or no missing dragons.

But I don't want to make the most of it. I just want to find Ziggy and Arthur.

Eddie

Dear Eddie,

I have just seen your messages. The Internet is a rare treat here in Tibet, but I managed to check my e-mails on a sherpa's phone.

Thank you for letting me know about the dragons.

You need not worry about Ziggy. She will be perfectly safe. Dragons are wise creatures, and she is even more sensible than most. She also has strong wings and powerful claws. I can't imagine anyone or anything in London will be a threat to her.

However, Arthur is quite different, and I am very concerned for his safety. A small dragon is not safe alone in a big city. He might have been run over or kidnapped or suffered some even more horrible fate.

I suggest you call the police and ask for their help.

I do hope you find them both soon, so you can enjoy your vacation in London. I have fond memories of the years I spent in that vast gray town. Few places could be more different than my current location: a cold, snow-covered mountainside in a remote region of Tibet.

We have had no confirmed sightings of the yeti, but I have arranged a meeting with a local shaman tomorrow, and I am hoping he will bring good news.

With love from your affectionate uncle,

Morton

THE DRAGONSITTER Series

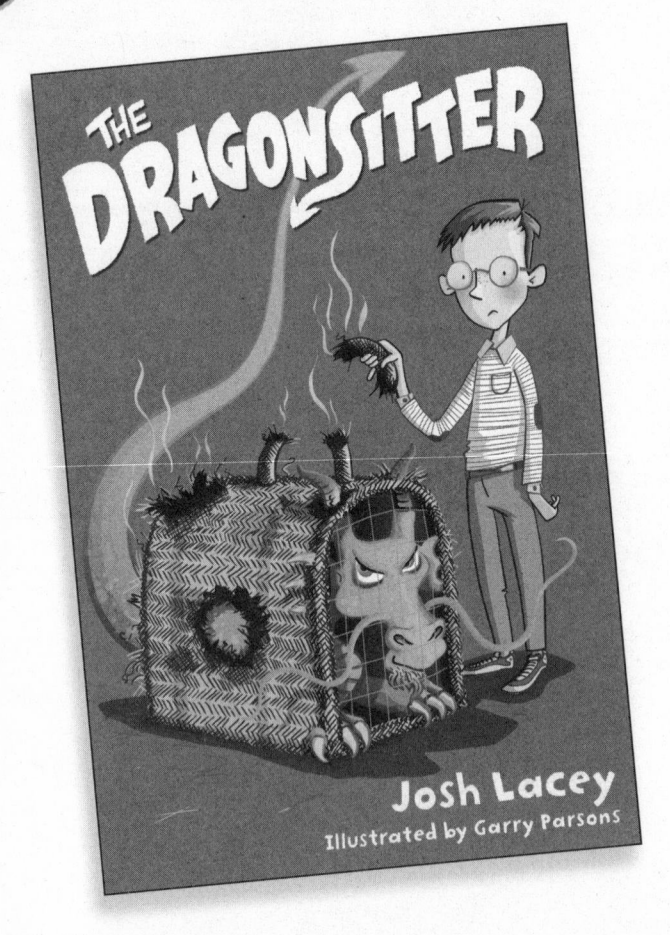

THE DRAGONSITTER

Josh Lacey

Illustrated by Garry Parsons

COLLECT THEM ALL!

If you enjoyed
THE DRAGONSITTER'S Party,
you might also like these series,

available now!

Don't miss a single **SPACE TAXI** adventure!

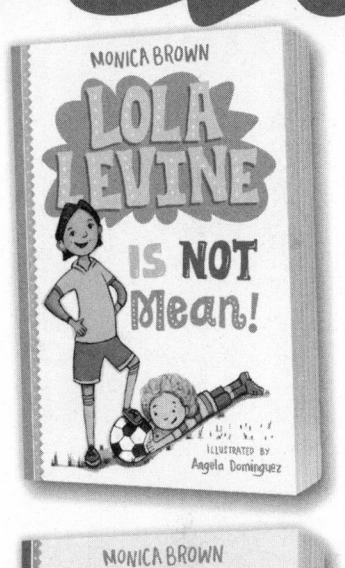

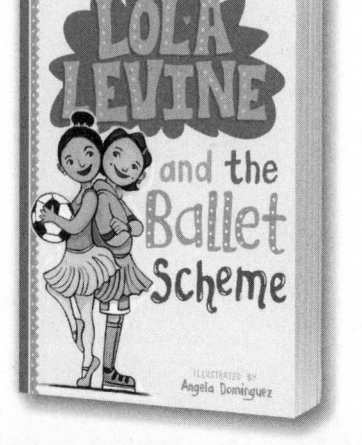

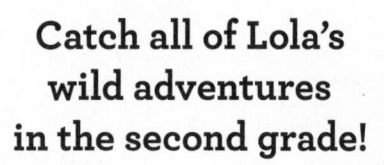